TRULY YOURS

Unsaid Me, Unheard You...

KRISHNA PANDA

Woven Words Publishers OPC Pvt. Ltd.

Registered Office:

Vill: Raipur, P.O: Raipur Paschimbar, Dist: Purba Midnapore,

Pin: 721401, West Bengal, India.

Branch Office (Operations): Hyderabad

www.wovenwordspublishers.com

Email: publish@wovenwordspublishers.com

First published by Woven Words Publishers OPC Pvt. Ltd., 2021.

Price: Rs.250/-

IMPRINT: WOVEN WORDS LAUNCHPAD

ISBN 13: 978-93-91213-00-8
ISBN 10: 93-91213-00-6

First Edition

Book size: 5*8

PROLOGUE

Dear Readers,

Penning this book has been a journey. If you are looking for any kind of motivation, inspiration, or any kind of business outlook then this book certainly doesn't address any of it. This book is intended to have a rendezvous tête-à-tête with you. In the hustle bustle of life, we tend to be a part of rat race to chase our goals. Well, isn't that's how life is to be lived! Wise men tell, "time and tide wait for none, and the show must go on". When the bizarre pandemic couldn't stop our spirit, then nothing in life could ever stop us. We as human species have this knack of adopting to every situation, invited or uninvited.

But.

We do also have a heart that just not carries our blood but also inestimable emotions which we somewhere tend to disregard or find trivial to address. So, with the wheels of time rolling fast, these emotions pile on and later take a back seat. No, there's neither grudge nor regret about why certain words were left unspoken, why some emotions were felt but were not indispensable enough to cling on, why certain feelings were felt at certain point in a certain way but were left unattended and unquestioned.

As an eventful day ends, we sit on our balcony and watch the fast-paced life, sipping a cup of coffee. I look to give you company through this book. Let just a leaf of this book take you to your epoch times when you were raw with your emotions and feelings. When that single glance could send jittery to your senses, and you became restless. When those unreasonable waits for someone, you know not why, made up your day. When there were many such 'when' moments which you and only your heart knows but never had the audacity to discuss. Read on, not with a motive to complete this book. Read on to live those moments and come back to life feeling completed.

This book is a coffee table read, a balcony night read, 30,000 feet above flight read and so on and so forth when you are a solitaire. This book is a time travel machine. Read on. I promise you to feel light after each page you live by yourself.

So why waiting, let's take a deep breath. Ladies and gentlemen, I present this book with an effort to discover yourself in the dungeons of memories and making up for all the lost times with your heart.

Take care of your heart! Read on.

GRATITUDE

Writing a book is harder than I thought and more rewarding than I could have ever imagined. I am eternally grateful to God for blessing me the best people of the world:

Maa and Bapa: I love you Maa and Bapa for giving me wings to fly and for being my strength. This life is your giving.

Chandan: I would like to thank you dear husband for being the winds beneath my flight. Know this, you are a part of my identity and I love you.

Nani and GJ: Thank you for giving me bundle of joys Naina and Lokesh.

Rehman: None of this would have been possible without you. Thank you for meeting me the very next day when I discussed of publishing this book without worrying about your safety during pandemic. That is true friendship.

A special thanks to all my readers, colleagues, friends, and well-wishers for being there in my creative pursuits. I am what I am is because of your good thoughts and support.

Dear God, needless to thank you. You are the scriptwriter of my life. I am just a mere artist playing roles defined by you.

Naina and Lokesh, 'Truly Yours' book belongs to you. A wise man once said, "The best thing you can gift to your children is a library". Hence, while you walk through Massi's designed library in future I would like you to pick up Massi's books and rejoice…

And one fine day, maybe if I have enough strength left within me, I shall write a book; the pages of which will ride you high to a greenery islet. Each word will float and create ripples in your mind. As you get engrossed with all that existed between us like the ifs, buts, no, yes, silence, hesitation, truth, lies et al, you will see your reflection in the book. I will use choicest of words that will sketch you in the most vivid and illustrious way. By the time you go through the last page of the book a tear drop from the moment will roll down from your eyes and settle on that page. O Sweet love of mine, love of thine shall be mine forever that moment.

CONTENTS

1. Confession 17
2. Wish 18
3. Music 19
4. Shelter 20
5. Rain 21
6. Date 23
7. Unknown 24
8. Togetherness 25
9. Introspection 26
10. Bygones 27
11. Retro Love 28
12. Invitation 29
13. Wonderings 30
14. Déjà Vu 31
15. Miracle 32
16. Ruminating 33
17. Agony 34
18. Clandestine 35
19. Quandary 37
20. Homecoming 38
21. Letter 39
22. Emotions 41
23. Abode 42
24. Coffee 44
25. Silence 45

26. Rains 46
27. Love 48
28. Moon 49
29. Grudge 51
30. Euphoria 52
31. In Betweens 54
32. Surrender 56
33. Question-I 57
34. Just 58
35. Salvation 59
36. Erased 60
37. Nothingness 62
38. Solitaire 63
39. Regret 65
40. A Magic Spell 66
41. Page 69
42. Cacophony 70
43. She 71
44. Connections 72
45. Numbness 73
46. Solace 74
47. Butterfly 75
48. Heart 77
49. Symphony 78
50. Longing 79
51. Ask Me Not! 81
52. Story 82
53. Night 84

54. Once 85
55. Gratitude 86
56. Realization 87
57. Beckon 88
58. Desires 89
59. Question-II 91
60. Sentences 93
61. Monologue 94
62. Elixir Of Life 95
63. Goodbye 96

CONFESSION

O beloved! Such is this heart's desire for you that shadow of your thoughts is home for the wanderer and your quest is discovering elixir of life. Where art thou!

Slow down a bit. Youth have reached the penultimate. Why is there a need to rush! Come near. Sit for a while. Evening is to stay before night dawns. Let's give life a miss. Don't we mean a world for each other? Pause for a while. Words that I swallowed over years are set to release on your lane. Give me a moment from your being. We are here. Let's stay for a while.

Understand path of love is topsy turvy. But Darling, we shall take the scenic route; the swinging slopy smooth route. Love, lets romance with each other's life. What say?! Let's rejoice life.

WISH

Sometimes how a caravan of words fail to pour out the feelings that lie dormant somewhere in the backyard of mind. Emotions mostly dormant by demeanor, often get active when the hot iron rod of memorabilia strikes the most sensitive chord of heart. It's in those moments I play the fondest and oldest ghazal in my gramophone, the one that has a relatively slower rhythm. The silent breeze traverse through the wild, reaches my window, tussle with the curtains and finally finds the way to caress my soul. Such is love.

The fingers today play like the notes of a piano as I sit to type an orphaned letter to you.

How I wish every letter I write float like a paper boat in a rain drenched night to the address of your heart. Sometimes I so wish my letters to you fly out of my window to your world like a careless light sheet of paper soaked in twilight aura.

Alas, my wish remained but just an unfulfilled wish.

So, my Love, I solace my heart hearing to the wind chimes ringing in lovers' glory. But cross my heart one fine sunny day when the lights set in, I shall pen every word that's truly yours!

MUSIC

Sometimes I stand on the Howrah Bridge. Not often. Sometimes. When the twilight is dressed as a bride in the sunken horizon, I stand waiting for the fisherman to put his last net on the river. In those sometimes I see an unknown man playing the flute at a distance enticing me in its rhythmic bits. Last evening, I saw that man holding a guitar and playing the chords in a tremulous way. Maybe it was his first time. Isn't it first time always a nerve-racking ordeal? Excitements, fear, enthusiasm all at one go synchronize to give the best rawness. Such were you and me! The first-time introvert lovers.

Unlike us, the bridge was gregarious ever since it met us. Bridges often serve to be connecting links between lovers, strangers, and unfamiliar voices. Music flows when the twilight zephyr caresses the surface of the river beneath the bridge.

The zephyr then brings along with it the unknown man's notes of flute. It is at this moment the music belongs to me and I am a part of you.

SHELTER

So soft and gentle are love tip toes that only the heart of a lover can hear. In a gallery where crowd echo much, the melodious symphony of love still discovers its way to the beloved. Love is like an orchestra. The louder it gets, the sensuously deep it plays with a lover's mind. At times love is the guiding pole star showing the rosy path to paradise.

The winds tonight make way beyond the curtains and the pages of the book flickers denying settling. The solitaire peeps out of the windows to see the sparkling moon. Enigma widens. The reflection of moon glisten on the river and the heart turns sonata. It is in that miraculous aura; the lover finds a shelter within his inamorata. They tell, "Love find its way to every heart like river finds the ocean."

As you flip through the pages of your diary tonight, I shall not reflect on your eyes. Tonight, I shall sparkle on your lips. Wear me in red, love!

Truly Yours

RAIN

Often this heart has wondered what happens in your part of the world when it rains! What sepia gheraos you when pale clouds cast shadows in your city!

When it rains in my side, I see that fatigued bullock cart or that trolley puller rushing back to their houses in haste. Perhaps they have earned enough *Rotis* to survive tonight. The kids on the street are playful with splashes from above. The two 'yet- to- confess- their-love' lovers take a refugee under the shed of a half roof tea shop to sip hot *matka* chai. You see, rain, love and the chills of tea, quite make up a heavenly combination! The girl all drenched is conscious of her flimsy wet tops, while the boy turns to gaze at the *Rabindro* Bridge that stands tall on the opposite side of the sea. The *Rabindro* Bridge well dressed in a divine attire of rainbow knows it all what's going between the two love birds. Soon the street gets waterlogged as rain perform in full sway.

The scribbler waits till then in her balcony. Her wetlands in her heart start harvesting with emotions of rawness, desire, passion, and fire. No more today she shall write through the ink of her blood. She looks at her inkpot with anticipation.

"This loneliness, this urging of "You", the talks that never happened between us but in my mind a zillion times, of

all that went un-noticed, uff, love, the rains are re-playing it all like gramophone.

Now tell me what the story in your part is."

DATE

Tonight, as I sit on the green lushes feeling the luscious whips of air in my senses, I realize moon has always been between you and me. Though our connection is strong but somewhere connection gets intertwined with the moon in between. Therefore, I have always loved the crescent moon with a lone star above it. For lovers like us the crescent moon has always been a symbol of romanticism. Unlike the full moon, the crescent moon has no dark mole on it.

I feel the silence in this cosmic aura. Tonight, in your absence your silence is connecting me with you. So, love, I beg of you, please be one with me tonight. You see, timeless is love and uncertain is time. I can't anymore trust on time, understand. Hold me close. Look! There shines the pole star ablaze. Let's walk in that direction. I shall lead you to the bonfire that burns with the passion of my love. Will you walk with me? They tell darkness and wilds are often too engrossing and enigmatic. But it also has serenity, tranquility, and the essence of silence. Virgin love takes birth in those places. Enticing is the aura there.

O you, tonight for once, I extend my hands, expand my arms wide, be my date tonight?!

UNKNOWN

Words are often betrayers. They conceal behind the cocoon of silence. A state of loneliness exists when words become oblivious. Loneliness and silence don't exist by choice. Like frozen lava the unexpressed emotions are the reason behind silence. Often the wall of silence stumble when heart melts while expressing. Therefore, some lines should be sans words. Hiding emotions from the world is easy. But not good enough for self!

Nobody knows the stories you have lived, the lives you have lived, the silences you have hidden. Nobody knows. Don't we reveal the most irrelevant part of ours!

She put her spectacles down, looked deep at the fizzles rising from bonfires, wrapped herself into the blanket, "Ah, nobody either knows a solitaire." She puts her diary into the bonfire and took her last breath witnessing her entire life in a jiffy on a grand screen running in front of her eyes. "Adieu, life."

TOGETHERNESS

Let not your thoughts fly tonight through the notes of guitar or symphony of melodious zephyr. Let not they come through the sip of my coffee on my lone desk or through the sea breeze from my windows. O you, let not it cross the distance of the echoes of faraway hills!

Between you and me let our thoughts today swing to and fro, ounce by ounce, caressing the wind chimes, making that clinging sound of temple's bell, unfurling the lilies and crafting the petals into a beautiful rose.

When the waves rest on the surface of the sea and the storm within turns dormant, I shall pluck the lilies and that lone rose sparkling in mystic aura of that moonbeam night to craft our togetherness into a magenta poem. On that night, it shall not be the ink of my inkpot that shall carve our togetherness on the white sheet, rather it shall be the hues of lilies and rose that will pen our togetherness poem. Cross my heart, the poem shall sparkle in the midst of darkness.

INTROSPECTION

Often my words sail to your island. Not in a hope of your return. O, do the passing breeze ever turn back? My words often peep into your windows. They say you still gaze at the moon; you pen some words in your black diary on your desk. That the love novel which made love knock at the doorstep of your heart still lies by your bed side, that the Kashmiri quilt veils you but lower to your heart. I know you still set your heart free and unveiled. Those words also do smile watching how the morning rays disturb your sleep. That they tell me you do, yes you do, sneak peek at me, like I do. But in my case, it's different. I tell my words to make sure all's fine with you. Don't know what's your part of story. It's okay some stories are better when left untold.

Anyways these words have made me realized nothing much has changed. I, the inconsistent lover and you, the lingering impression.

BYGONES

Strange is love. It’s not about just that one person. Eons after when nostalgia hits the shore, it’s not about that person. Equations have changed, memories have faded, and you feel no more. You just remember. Remember that one person like the ground remember that uprooted dead tree.

But.

That feeling. That which you felt once upon a time remains even more special. That makes your heart beat fast when moistened nostalgia filled breeze touch your heart.

Yes, now love is, but that exceptional feeling, you felt once. It was never about that only person.

RETRO LOVE

Sepia flashes today. O Sweet love of mine, this heart is not mindful without you. It keeps to and fro between twilight dreams of Howrah bridge to mud cup of hot tea on that dusted bench. That old library where I watched you in between book racks runs in my mind today. Oh, there were many in between us! Isn't it? You were always my last head turn after college got over and your name the last on the ending page of my notebooks. The metros ran fast. But those metros that took me to meet you was special.

This heart races still the same. Silence still echoes, the hesitation in our eyes still the same. But time all the more different...

O sweet love of mine, in you I find a home. I have taken many a boat built with poetry just to meet you on sultry nights. So, you see, the wait still the same. Just look around, ahead of you, I am at the other end of Howrah. Seal the distance between us. Stitch all the 'between' so that not last page we deserve a fairy tale in front page of our life story.

INVITATION

Come let's go to the other side. Without any question, let's give the day a miss. This world has been too dubious. Let's settle somewhere far from the monotony, let lie for a while near the calm river, on the moistened earth, wrapped with the zephyr, under the sacred turquoise sky, in a day light, no moon to stare, no stars to count, the sun also shall be veiled with the clouds, yeah, you got it right, it should be a no-show day for all the celestials. As we lie watching the vastness of azure, do not speak a word, they take most of the time. Instead, let nothing come between. Let's just take deep breathes and close our eyes.

Shhh...No, let the moment head us to it. I rest my pen here. Feel it. Are you feeling me?!!

WONDERINGS

Over the years I have often wondered what you are to me!? True that, as you say, 'Not necessary all relations need to have a name' but I have realized one thing, you are my 'escape zone'. Often when this world is too much to handle, I walk back to you, your arms my safety blanket and the idea of you is solace to this heart.

Isn't that we say what a soulmate is all about?! But there you go again, "let's not think, let's not argue, it's a divine intervention, it's cosmic connection!"

So, for tonight, let your Charmer play the flute, you weave poetry and syllables and as usual the Moon witness our symphony through the rustling branches.

In an alien world, in another time there won't be further between you and me. If any, there will be, just and only, you and me having enough of each other, till then let's hold on to the Cosmic connection.

In Gratitude,
Forever.

DÉJÀ VU

So soft and pristine is the touch of morning zephyr today that it feels like love from past has visited after eons or a love from womb of hope is about to come to its form. The birds today celebrate magnanimity singing hymns of epoch and assured tomorrow.

The silence so loud and the peace so visible that the heart feels it. The ticktock of clock so still today as if a moment just dropped from the high tide that took a turn shying away from the morning sun.

Yes, Love speaks today.

MIRACLE

Dear Beloved,

As the night turn grey today hold my dreams in your eyes. For once, let me see how love and dreams merge at the wake of dawn in beloved's eyes. O you. let not weave words tonight! Hold me close. Let witness the fusion as the miracle unfurl.

Ask me what magic is!

A blissful night,
a pinch of love,
a sensuous coffee,
a window of solitude,
a restful chair,
twisted captivating thoughts,
echoing silence.
Uh! I have had enough of you.

Ahoy!
Truly Yours

RUMINATING

You take my word and begin your lines. Well, isn't that's how you caught a writer's attention! That's how we started communicating and that's how our silences are now communicating. Isn't it wonderful all through these years of what we are to each other and how it's progressing! So what, we are not talking about it. Darling, know this, things that are instinctively felt are rarely expressed and often left unspoken. Because the heart knows it all. You, yes You, do you get it?!

When someday I become a passing wind and blow through your world, stop me for once to feel. I will stop, I promise. When one day the sky shall rain without signs of any clouds and you feel like to embrace life, I promise, I will be that one of your rains drenched night. That night wishes me to stay longer. Cross my heart, I shall rain incessantly. And someday, if you want to see Sun and moon together close your eyes and whisper my name. Understand not all that are felt meant to be seen and that which are seen are not meant to be lived.

AGONY

Nobody knows how far a blank stare goes. How many words someone's silence is. How much a tear weigh. How wide a smile is. How deep feelings are. Yet in all their assumptions, life stands witness of what should have been, could have been and will be.

Yesterday it rained. Inside out. From heart to eyes. From dungeons of memories to gullies of yesteryear. Between you and me. From hi to bye and till sighs. Amidst silence. In clandestine moments and veiled quilt. On soaking pillows and from why 'this' to how 'it has to be'. From dreams to deliriums. Within moments of longing for presence to absence. It rained, stained, pained, and drained.

CLANDESTINE

There is something that's making me smile today. It's like waking up to a spring morning where every creation seems to be perfect in its divine order. The world today appears pristine to eyes as if last night it has been drenched by holy milky showers from clouds of rainbow reverie. Is it you behind this unusual smile?

I exactly can't fathom that moment when I fell for you. It was a spur of moment. Oh, it didn't take long. Just by the time the skylark spread its wings and flew from one branch to another of the same tree, my heart skipped from my space to yours and suddenly, my world started trembling. How could it not be? You were about to be my world. I started having a secret conversation with moon. Usually, stars did sometimes join us If not anyone, pole star in between oft joined us.

Love defies all logic. My mind was losing its battle of 'what it knew' to 'what it felt'. The western winds blew in all its mighty force. Storm passed by. I defeated all of them. Then a whip of air passed by. So soft and delicate was its feel that it almost caressed my soul. You walked in briskly. The story was just about to begin…

… And then something within me whispered to you, "You will never know, you in my life is like having a secret affair with the moon."

Truly yours.

QUANDARY

There's something I want to tell you today after meeting you. I don't know what I want to tell you. But. These are those words that are meant just for you. Those words that are only between you and me. That I have never told you. Actually, I feel like I told you manifold times. In many ways, in many words, in myriads dialects, in numerous styles, in oceanic silence, in various art forms. No, I am sure I told your that day. But what did I tell you that I need to tell again?

There's something I want to tell you today. Words today fly like butterfly dreams, unwilling to settle in my nameless verse. They fly to a distant undiscovered island. Reluctant, hesitant, unwilling, untamable, inscrutable they are.

Not that your thoughts often bewilder me, but they are not that distracting today. So, tell me O you, what is that which I am not able to recall!

The birds will soon begin their flight. Twilight will soon bid an adieu. And. Words will soon disappear in randomness. All my somber heart knows is that it got to spell out some magic as the words flow from my lips.

Plead you dear birds, sing me your song!

Let the rain play the notes of mystic. They say memories often come alive in such canonical hours. Before the dusk sets in, let me steal a lifetime from both our lifespan. This life is nothing but a saga of you and me. But what is that which I want to tell you today?

HOMECOMING

So delicate and tender are your homecoming is that only my heart can sense; like the bells of Church, like the silent fast heart beats of that first confession, like that temptation when sprinkles from heaven touch the virgin leaves.

When that sharp lightening rises amidst the clouds to draw the sky into two, my heart start pouncing and skipping like an infant. The zephyr of the dark tempest night then play a soothing glorious music and I rush to my balcony to see if the moistened winds this time have brought you along. I see, but the kids playing to their heart's mirth in rain-soaked street. The nightingale sings her first love song while the yellow page diary falls off the shelf bringing back the bygone era when our looks were first exchanged. Nostalgia revisits as if an old almirah filled with rust and dust opens with treasure. The parched pale effervescence rose of yore no longer seek to be within the flickering silent pages. Tonight, it wants to stand witness to *us*. So, love, hold me tonight close before my heart chooses to fly like that colorful kite of festive seasons, for love's nest is in the abode high.

Can you sense me, O you? Tonight, I wait your homecoming.

LETTER

Dear You,

Spanking new dawn, pristine sky, immaculate air, aromatic aura and here I am, with a wide smile and unruffled look. Your thoughts tip toes and lean on my mind. Is it what they call magic? Often, without you, I have spoken a zillion word to you. I wonder how you never knew them when you read my heart so well. May be my words are gibberish or inefficient to convey my feelings to you. But darling, love never knows any language! Language is, but an illusion to create spaces through misinterpretation. Listen to me in silence. Feel me with the sprinkling, splashing invisible dew drops of zephyr. Read those unspoken words that are beyond full stops, comas, ellipses, semicolons, or any other punctuations. You know writing to you is like searching for that lone blossom on the top of a faraway hill. The blossom is an impossibility and so are you. You have an enduring charm that draws me towards you, and I know not why! A hopeless dreamer now I am turned to, wishing for you, my lone Michelangelo wish. Since the day we have met, mornings have turned to dreamy nights, hours into minutes and minutes into manifold moments of intimacy. I treasure all of them somewhere very deep within me. What more! Words often pay heed and reject me in the best way when I think of you. The first time I felt your presence, this heart felt like home in a rain drenched sultry deserted night.

Truly Yours

EMOTIONS

Emotions often are Casanovas. They drive our adrenaline crazy. In a sultry night when a lover peeps at the vast azure the Casanova emotions climb the ladder of reminisces to settle on moon and paint blur images. Most times they take form of a boat tied to a sail in a far-off land and at times sketching a bridge connecting two ends. They are also an unknown road divulged into two, the traveler unsure which path to take. Winter emotions are of the withered leaves in purple, maroon and red, fallen from *deodar* on an orphaned road. Like withered leaves emotions often look for life to go back in time! Summer emotions are like that thirsty bird and unfathomable well in a remote place where that bird's thirst and distance seldom meet.

Sigh! Emotions give birth to memorabilia which the poet stores in an old almirah or treasure it in a box. Lovers keep them in between pages of diary sealed with a drop of tear fallen from a moistened moment.

Life, in its uncanny way, in its unusual gregarious approach keeps flowing in-between the fist. The more we try to hold, the more it slips in between. What remains are these emotions- the phoenix that rises from the ashes of time.

Emotions are omnipotent. Vouch on any lover!

ABODE

I have always tried innumerable times to stop giving shape to strangest emotions and thoughts. My aim is to dispose them in a blank sheet and giving them a death of nomad. Yes, a nomad. They rise from distant moods, taking a dig into my daily life and suddenly when I think of erasing them, they disappear to some other day and keep coming on and forth. At times they make me envy. Why can't I be like them? Appear and disappear as per my wish without a clue. People would never search me knowing that someday like these nomad thoughts and emotions, the return is a must.

This process of writing is also quite uncertain. When I think of beginning to pen my emotions, the pen denies moving citing me the reason of having way off with words. Words and emotions make a great bond, I tell you. They hold me like a pendulum and make me move to and fro. At one point, there is silence and at the other end, there is be-wilderness. I try hard not to move in their directions, taking refuge in the position of rest. By rest I mean numbness. A numb heart gives solace. Where everything fuses with nothing. Where silence, nothingness, loneliness, darkness, noise, screams, pace, a full stop, coma, ellipse all seem to be one full circle.

Out of all the memories that have been treasured in the old box, few images flash in my mind when the pen starts its journey. The sight of a sunset. Then it's the sight of a lonely boat somewhere amid fortunes. Sands of time remind me that the vagabond journey will find its direction in its rippling breezes and waves. I too shall reach my own island. How strange is that! Hoping against hope! Is it this what we call as optimism?

Sometimes I envy the wet leaves after rain. Can I ever be like them- wet, fresh, brand new, breathing pure air, washing away all the dusts of the past from my life's surface.

So listen dear you, there are times when these thousand absurd thoughts strike me, when life keeps me too busy to find my way back to me, when I am lost in my riddle, when I tend to be a wanderer seeking self-discovery, when I am oscillating between simile, metaphor, sonnets and what not! Hold my hand and make me yours. I shall find a home. Home within you.

Truly Yours.

COFFEE

My art of making coffee is just as old as my love for you. The mastery of this art goes as deeper and skillful as days pass by with your love. The taste of coffee sometimes varies like your mood swings, but I make sure the color stays as deep as your hairs. I paint your eyes on the top of the coffee with a smile like the first time you met me. Ah! A slice of sugar is enough to give that sweetish relish to soul, for your words were often too blunt to digest. But in all ways, I love the coffee like the way I love you. My sumptuous coffee is mostly as hot as your lips and the creamy dollop of foam topping is as seductive as my desire for you. The fumes that rise from the cup makes me lie down as you rise high on me, caressing my cheeks, going upward, downward, in all its twists and turns, giving me that lush feeling. Enough! Let me have the coffee before you sensualize me.

O beloved! Such is this heart's desire for you that shadows of your thoughts are home for the wanderer and your quest is discovering the elixir of life. Where art thou!

SILENCE

Irony of love is that it teaches silence to be louder and words to be silent. Silence often has been a great respite since the day I saw you. I know not how to express. I know not how to convey. I know not how to show. They say silence is enough. But. Distance? How does this silence traverse the hill of distance to reach you?

Sometimes I wonder do silences echo? Had it been, then O you tell me, how many times did it wake you up from your dreams? Or did they ever make place in your dreams?

Silences have made me a lost traveler. I wait for words. I look for them to discover me. Words these days do not travel in vacuum. They flow from my inkpot, spill on the paper and make a rippling effect in my mind. All storms begin with a silence. A violent whirlpool stupefies the aroma. Silence plays its flute. Often in those times, I sit near my lone chair on the balcony and watch the twilight evade in the vicinity of horizon. *Sans a word. Sans you. Along silence. Along the thoughts of you.*

May winds, you know! They bring too much of you. Blame the silence of the night and warmness it carries; they make me somewhat incomplete without you. I don't know, but. You see, even May says, "I am full of unsurety."

RAINS

The rain poured in into the tiny poles of the parched heart of earth. Sleekness gave a soothing feeling that quenched the thirst of eon old. The lover in the umbrella struggled to get cozy.

"Rains often bring two poles nearer under one shade", thought she, holding her cell phone in an attempt to capture that moment of hesitation. Often the best snaps are the one that capture moments rather than shots. When life goes too far beyond our imagination those albums of memorabilia express the ditto emotions felt then.

She held the rain in her hands.

He went on. "No, we were not those typical lovers. Never went on a date or spent quality times. We talked, shared our feelings. I do think of her. But. We were not in love. We admired each other."

The lightening smashed the ceilings. The night was filled with grudges. Grudges of rain for the time it had to stay distant from the earth. Love knows no separation. Distance bring storm along with it. The desperation triggers the devastating storm.

"Love has a place in dreams and life has to be practical. I cannot match her standards. I have my

setbacks and weaknesses. I have people to be answerable to. Hence I gave love a sacrifice."
She thinks in wild imagination," Sacrifice? What good it brought? No difference to family but pain to your heart. Excuses in love is absolute betrayal."

"I don't think of her. I don't love her. It all ended. We are away from each other. That's all."

She smiled back.

There is a gap between falling in love and being in love. The one who covers the gap has a story to tell. The one who doesn't, has memories to hold on.

He confessed to his heart those that he never said in all the years, "I never wanted you to go. Even though there was nothing to exchange, not even words or blank stare. I just wanted time to pass by while we sit. I wanted you to 'just be' and 'never to leave'. You understand what that mean?!

LOVE

Make me your verse tonight if you cannot make me yours. At least when you pen me, I will sparkle in your eyes and be the sweet murmur of your lips. O you, I don't know why but I am madly in love tonight. I did let you go to set my heart free from love. Little did I knew the free heart shall find way back to you. Ask me what love is! Love is the tussle between you and me. The more I distance from you, the more I find myself within you. The moon, the stars, the sky, the vast azure, everything reminds me of you. What is this symphony of saxophone that play all around me in sleepless nights? Is it you? If love is worship, then I am your worshipper. If love is silence, then I am the Saint chanting your hymns. If love is wild, then find me in those sparks of bonfires that frizzles to awaken passion.

O you, Yes, I do! I am madly in love. With you.

Truly Yours.

MOON

It was a rarest full blue moon night. Clouds acted as shield to the moon. The whiter the clouds, the bluish the moon was. A wild aura seduced the night. Moon in bits and pieces appeared to him amidst the rustling leaves. The perfect harmony he was seeking for many years.

Chapter of love has begun. So, the restlessness was instinct. The peacock feathers couldn't suffice his growing yearning. Ah! Love. So addictive is the bite of love.

He conveys his words through his eyes, "You know how it is moon? Sometimes I want to steal her from her realm and hide her in my heart and before she could say something seal her lips with a kiss."

He lay on his bed. The vast azure seems mystical. The Venus sparkling the best and there she was, her inamorata from that world sprinkling her love in all directions. He smiles and keeps the letter he wrote to her once, long before she existed, beneath his pillow. The letter worded, "don't meet me in dreams tonight. My plan is to abduct you forever."

The moon peeps out of the clouds chuckling, "I shall read someday, all those letters from you to her."

He whispers, "Good night, moon. Spend the best night because I am having one."

GRUDGE

He peeped out of his window as the breeze caressed his heart. The soothing feeling filled the silence with ecstasy. It was cold out but warm within him. He closed his eyes for a minute. Sometimes it becomes so necessary to cut off from the unnecessary world.

He pens in his heart some words gibberish because tonight his mind and heart were not in his hold.

"Give me that glance, those quick breathes you took when I was around, those unspoken immaculate words between us, that pristine luscious zephyr making way between us, those silent hours when I couldn't have you enough, those conversations that happened often in minds, those nights when sleep eluded me. O you, can you gift me all that and beyond? Sigh! Here I stand the vagabond wishing nothing more than a smile, for just a thought that once you were all mine is in itself the best gift I ever had."

Krishna Panda

EUPHORIA

There is something in today's dawn that I am shivering and feeling the chill within. Last night it rained inevitably, and the moon was nowhere to be seen. My inkpot was almost dry and the uncapped pen which often penned me was reluctant. Last night therefore I slept not with my everyday dreams but with your thoughts. Exclusively your thoughts that I hold so fondly in some tiny corner of my heartless chest. Today I feel a strange sense of fragrance embracing me. I am enticed sans any sorts of addiction. Is this called falling in love! In the wee hours as I look beyond the sea, I think of you. Yeah, you. Expressive eyebrows and those daunting romantic eyes, I tell you, it kills me often in my wildest dreams. Words often pay heed when I try to make sense while conveying my feelings to you. I am drawn towards you like that gibberish song sung by a distant solitaire which often hold my attention. I was a jittery soaked, drenched, and drowned in my own mysticism when I came across you. Merely at your touch, compassion, romanticism, sui generis persona, the frozen soul within me started melting. So here I am standing on the bridge, a redefined me.

Let's meet today in the twilight aura, here on the Howrah Bridge. Bridge, they tell connects two ends and evokes a manifold poetry. Today I would dress up in the simplest attire for it's your presence that will illuminate me. You just come to lighten the twilight before dusk cast a spell. We will watch together the sunset point and make some wish. They say a wish at sunset often comes true. You make a wish and my only wish, you know, is all your wishes should come true. We will not talk about love. Love often makes one restless and emotions cause a rush in the adrenaline. We will not see each other. Down the bridge when the fisherman spreads out the last net on the river, we will look at each other, only for once. Kolkata's adrak wali tea in matkas, I tell you, it's something to drool at. As the lights spark the Howrah Bridge and the twilight gets dimmer, I and you will expressively smile besides those zillion smiles that we often hide from each other ever since we met.

I shall be optimistic today for I would give myself no other choice. You see the togetherness we share inspite of all tumults, I and You must today rise in love instead of falling.

And today if we don't meet, then know this, come what may, if even we part ways or tomorrow for some reason if you hate me, you will forever remain dearest to my heart and irreplaceable.

IN BETWEENS

Some mornings are like those first blossom unfurling life in the wake of dawn. They fill your heart with warmth of that effervescent fume that rises whimsically from your favorite coffee mug. You take a deep breath almost absorbing the whole of life. A state of wordlessness, nothingness, void, calmness, quietude sets in, and you are in an unexpected trance. You open the leaves of yesteryears, visit the once upon a time lived era, touch the space of known and unknown, desired and undesired, lived and dreamt, loved and yet to be loved. You experience a great emotional shift. The breeze then mildly, in the most tender way makes love with your virgin heart, and you are sunk in the mystical era. As enigma seduces your mind and soul, you cross the lines of logic and limits. Later you wonder when did logic and limits defined you at all! All this while you have lived life on your own terms and conditions, sometimes like that ambitious bird soaring high trying to touch zenith and at times like a butterfly wishing someone somewhere would just want you to be with them sans any condition, commitments, names, bondage and an unsaid promise to be forever. One with whom you can hold on to life.

The intensity deepens. Something frozen starts melting.

Love has been a distant dream by now. It's like when love knocked at your door you were too busy and now when you have time for love, it just absconds. Then your attention falls on a book you read most recently. You know how it is, sometimes you choose a book to read and very rarely a book chooses you as a reader to answer all your questions. You are settled with the sought-after answers. You are aware. The universe has its very distinctive style of communicating with you. The sun peeps amidst the pillows of hills as if asking you, 'dear if you are done with your dreams and deliriums, can we begin our day!' You smile sluggishly and murmur, there is no escape to reality'.

SURRENDER

Let the exquisite cushion spread across the galaxies, let the meteors lighten the night , let the stars sing the oracles of longing love, let the moon keep me awake whole night, I will weave dreams of hopes, of possibilities, of reunion, of rekindled passion, of ignited whims and fantasies , of you , of me , of us. O love, do not explain logic. Thy love defies all logic. This heart is now a bird staying in the nest of your heart. It no more knows any of me. It tweets, chirps but only of you and about you. If this madness is love, yes, I am into it. I surrender.

QUESTION-I

Dear Love,

When it lightens, somewhere it rains. Papers of the diary have shaped to boat and sold to rain. I stand at the primrose path of life wondering what we lost or gain in time.

You have my words said, unsaid, implied, and avoided. I have fistful of your silence, grudges, and regrets. Of what we never had was a common door to our heart. But trust me in between our castles we had a common window. That window through which sunshine illuminated our soul. There's a cosmic connection between you and me, now and then.

Time when we tussle against time, when we peeped out to stare at moon, when I and you crossed each other's thought at least once a day, did we gain or lose?

What did we lose even after gaining? In the platform of life, I and you will cross each other's path manifold times. Come let's stop for tonight. Let's reside in our memorabilia. Shhh...You don't say a word. Tonight, lets our heart do the talk.

Truly Yours.

JUST

When silence settles on wet dew drops, sometimes I wish to call you back, just like that. Like that boy who sits on lawn in a sultry night awaiting the falling star to fulfill his wish, I wish to call you back. Like that girl who stares at blank azure during twilight or just as moon wishes on a luminous sky, I wish you to call back. Trust me when I tell *just like that.*

Ask me what it is to wait?! A lone window and deep breath shall reveal a saga. Ask me what it is to love?! The wet seat under the streetlight shall speak aloud.

Not all stories have a beginning, nor do they have an end. Not all tears have pain to share nor does all silence carry a storm. They are just. They are just a lump in throat which echoes beneath the wordlessness feeling of a pillow.

Perhaps today I will hold all heaviness close to heart. Seal them and if it rains next autumn, I will sell them to the gigantic oceanic storm.

At least to that day, come back to me. For once.
Forever.

SALVATION

Slight drowsiness in milky drenched morning is silky in its feel. The heart often unfolds in such moment. Petal of possibilities embraces the magical moments that universe offers with open hands.

Flaps of eyes unfurls from last dream. I find you by my side like a silkworm in its cocoon. I trickle my fingers tenderly into your oceanic hairs. You make slight wavy moments but not much.

Last night when you slept, I had plucked few stars to embellish in your hairs. Crescent moon dazzled in between your brows. How beautiful was it then! A moment ceased. Your lips were almost parched awaiting a kiss to fulfill its thirst. And. My vagabond lips were just enough to suffice to it. Passion ignited. Whilst night grew wild with each tick tock of clock, we discovered new island in each other. The contour of your cravings found its direction when I navigated your deep driving desires like a mariner.

Now as morning awakens, you will soon be a butterfly. Isn't love's glory in freedom?
Set you free!

Truly yours.

ERASED

The night is approaching soon, and a dark shadow is surrounding the desert of my heart. May be, it's the last storm it will be facing. After all, how long can it have its awful days? The sand can hold the rainwater for a certain span of time but someday the sands have to meet their fate; eventually someday the sand will be overpowered by the rain, and washed away by the rain. Likewise, tell me, oh dear, how long will I live with your memories? Where art thou in this vast universe? Your memories are fast getting eroded from my world and I can't stop but witness such famine. Where are you? I need your help to change my world, to embellish my heart with your wind chimes, to color my heart with fluorescent red and make it zestful by bringing cupids again into my love world. Oh dear, can you listen to my whimpers?

The pages of my diary have filled up to the brim. Each page tells a story about you and awaits your touch to give them life even after knowing the veracity that you will never return to read them. They are stifling. Perhaps they will die tonight. Look, even moon doesn't come to visit me often. Why should it come? It knows that the dreams we both once built together are all shattered, and he has no place in it. The moon asks me often that why didn't you turn back once. Wait! Why am I asking you question? The reason might be this is my last letter to you. The words in my diary will die tonight and so will my feelings. The decision is taken. I will burn my diary and those letters that you never read. What's the need to keep them close to me when I know that you will never read it, nor will they ever set me free from your memories? Yes, I need freedom…freedom from you. I loved you to hell, but you could never comprehend it. Living with you was impossible and living without you is also impossible. So, tell me darling, what should I do?

You left no other choice than to stay off from you. There came a moment when there were just two options- loving you or to choosing life over you? And I had to choose life over you because my life is just not my life. Oh, how can I ever forget it's you who once told me that 'love is never done at the cost of others?' How can I forget your precious words? Perhaps, this was the best lines I take along with me.

Nevertheless, it's raining here. I mean, the sky is raining. Not me. This heart only bleeds now. Tears have lost its way. What I am going to do now is to bring a matchstick and burn the diary and all those letters that I once penned for you. Know what? All that love taught me was that love begins with a tear and ends with a tear in eyes. So, mind you, no matter how far you run away from me, you are trapped in my eyes and will forever reside there. Goodbye…stay well where you are. Period.

NOTHINGNESS

I believe there comes a point in life when you are just fine. You can sit under the open sky and look at stars for a good enough time without needing anyone's company. You are in love with your silence. You can write incessantly without even thinking of anything or any instance in life. You are one with self. I call this an equilibrium state. Nothing to disturb you. Not taking anything deeply. Infact not thinking anything at all. A perfect state of nothingness. Stoic silence. The blades of fan doing the rounds and artificial air caressing the silent aura in deep dark room with thin rays of light making way between the gaps of windows. If people come, embrace them. If they go, keep the door open. But allow no reasons or emotions to make room during exit and entry. Life is best lived in between the moments of silence. But then mind asks, "Why silence?" The heart replies with a sigh, "Because it's not like I don't have anything to say. It's just that I have given up on speech."

SOLITAIRE

I love nights more than you. Unlike you, it never hesitates. It's a passage between you and me. It makes the world sleep, the street and lanes silent, the moon as watchdog to stillness and the fog to cover the eyes of the hills in the backyard of my abode. It serves as communion between my thoughts and your hesitations. Through it I have often treaded to your world of emotions and in those moments, I have fallen for love. You know what, you were always a part of me. Just that, knowing you, love happened, just like that. Yes, just like that.

Tonight, the dark hill behind my abode symbolizes a solitaire. It makes me realize that it is as lonely as I am, tonight. Only a solitaire can give the best company to another solitaire in moments when everything seems to be so perfect, when even the breeze hesitates to disturb the sultry leaves. The aura tonight echoes, 'let the stillness prevails'. Pathless, random, disorder words have finally surrendered to my fatigued fingers accepting to settle down on my plain sheet of paper. Trust me when I tell, poetry and I have parted ways since time immemorial. It reminds me of You. You, who is nowhere in the vicinity. They say 'You' now only exists in the musings of Between You and Me and in the midway of the silence in those trembling words when spelt. I fear nothing these days because I am a solitaire. They say, eeriness exists only when we are afraid of losing the best we have, and I am nowhere near my best. I am out of my comfort zone. I am willing to take risk, and steadily I am accepting the fact that I am evolving into a better person. Is it you behind this evolvement? Is it your thought beneath my silence, behind my quietude?

Holding my poetry book, I walk tonight bare foot on a path filled with fallen cadaver Deodar leaves. Don't know why but I want 'you' to listen to my poetry first. Tread into my dreams. I shall not recite them but whisper them in your ears. If by any chance, I fall asleep in your arms, make sure, you close my book. I don't want the breeze to even sense those poetry before your eyes make love with my poetry.

REGRET

I know not how to begin my lines. Always have struggled with an approach, a beginning, a start. I wish I could call out loud. I wish you could hear me for once. Only once. Just once. Love often leaves us cold from within. You know silence is easy. Expression is difficult. With you both of them are now impossible. A writer's fate is that she is cursed with power of speech and blessed with pen. When the midnight lamp lightens, it is me who burns to shape you into a muse. Read my eyes someday. Eyes has the veracity unlike tongue. Rains in my heart have grappled to tell you my stories but alas you never could understand any. I knew then you can never. Ask me what it is to hate someone. I have tried to hate you a million and one times every night but ended of falling for you every morning. You are someone I so madly want from distance. You will never understand because you are unable to understand what lies beyond what is seen. Now that we have a huge iceberg of differences, silence, so called hatred and 'avoid' tags between us, it has been even more difficult to confess what I always wanted to tell you.

I carry this in my heart, a part of truth, you will never know, and I could never say, until we meet in some other place, if there is any.

A MAGIC SPELL

The first sight when we met all seemed so pleasant. Love was in the air with sky turning red and birds chirping aloud flying high just like this evening. You stole the limelight like the diamond sparkling amidst darkness. I was losing my heart and soul to you without you making any effort. Wonderful hypnotizing words flowing from your beautiful heart was making me lost in a dream world leaving me addled. Crazy was what I turned after that, finding you everywhere. Yes, some unknown pristine feelings that I never felt before were swaying me towards you. The world unexpectedly turned to a heaven for me, and I started appreciating everyone. I could see nothing else than beauty. Somewhere, a story was being written by the zephyr when you and I watched the sunset point together standing on that bridge unaware of the fact that those were the eternal moments that would sustain us during our solitary times. Slowly as the days passed, I knew all good things in life come to an end. But still couldn't find guts to speak to you when moments were many. The day came, and we had to drift apart. You looked at me & all I could murmur was," Can you not read my eyes?" Life took a U-turn when the next morning I woke up and found a magic. You left your spirit within me and turned me to a starlet overnight. Still I lament not saying you a word. Atleast 'THANKS'. Now what I am is because of you.

Don't know whether it's your fault or mine or Time or Destiny or Unseen force! I still couldn't figure out the reason of abnegation of our mutual clandestine feelings. But days spent with you will always remain cherishable and will be treasured in my heart till death and may be after that. You and me on that lighted bridge, those crazy fun filled talks, serious future plans, manifold dreams that we dreamt, all makes me nostalgic today. Yes, I miss you a lot in each breathe I take.

The river and the trees today here are so silent. Brownie, my dog who so fondly loves you no more bark with joy when I come to the bridge now. May be, they all miss you like I do. Today I am reminded of the last smile I saw on your face which was priceless. Memories float when the fragrance of your thoughts brought sensation in my heart, and I could sense you by closing my eyes. I do still feel the same. You are in me always but not you, rather in disguise the MAGICAL SPELL that keeps my charm alive.

Now things are not like they used to be once, but I am still like the same old tree indifferent to change. People say I have grown up. I wonder what has grown up- I or my love for you? May be both. They say I don't talk too much now. But how would they know your invisible presence keeps me so much pre-occupied that I hardly notice their presence. Sometimes, you leave me awe stuck. Do you have any idea that your invisible presence fills your absence in my life?

Anyways, I may not have my cheers but certainly have my tears. Here's a wish coming from core of my heart to you and just for you:

"Hope, never you forget smiles for I will die from miles"

It's time now for moon to arrive. I must go back to home. Tomorrow is special. Special for me. Like always this time also I will be on that glistening bridge, looking at the bright moon holding the red rose, closing my eyes, wearing a serene smile, wishing my only wish to you - HAPPY VALENTINE'S DAY. They say telepathy rocks.

But then there goes an old saying, "if you can't read my silence, how can you understand my words." No, don't think I am complaining. Felt like it stands true for both of us. Sometimes I question myself 'what's my status'? Single, Committed, Broken heart.

May be a SILENT LOVER....oops!
Let me put in this way....'Unexpressed'.

If ever you think to visit me then please note my new address. Yeah! I have shifted from Dream world to Utopia. Thanks so very much for spreading radiance in my life.

My secret unrequited crush.

Truly Yours.

PAGE

And sometimes how wonderful life seems to be. The world sleeps while you are awake. Silence with not a speck of dust to make movement. Life opens like an interesting novel in the mid of somewhere. I rapidly turn back the pages and images start dancing on the immaculate pages. The mystifying aura, that fragrance filled hazy singing night, the inviting swans, the almost shy unfurling lotus, that peeping of nightingale from the leaves of oak , the seductive breathes, that almost heard pouncing beats of hearts, the hesitating smiles and almost visible feelings…Ah! Each moment are treasures to be relished, cherished, and worshiped, for those were the culmination of the memories made when I lived my life. A slice of air then brings on to the page where 'YOU' began in my life. I blink my eyes with acceptance. Yes, the deep ferocious silence within me is the replica of my love for you. I know it's in my silence when I love you the most. The noises are just an excuse to want you but in silence you reside within me. Don't know what love is. Well, life and time never gives me chance to ponder over matters of heart. So, on your page I add on to this - "Love is but only YOU. Period." And then the book of my life disappears.

CACOPHONY

And then love asked to beloved, "*who am I to you?*"

The beloved in silence looked the moon direction. With eyes full of aqua replying in a broken voice and almost cold within, "You will be always that tear in my eye that rolls down during solitude. You are the voice of my solitude. That ache which is incurable. That thirst the ocean can't sustain. Yeah, you are that part of vast azure I can never belong. The star fish dazzle under moonlit sky and my love dazzle when the world turns numb. The frozen silence sometimes speaks too much. Do not listen to what they speak. Listen to the pauses the frozen silence take. If possible, listen to the lucid breath they take after completing a line or a word. Sometimes hold my cushions, quilt or my pillows, they will narrate what you mean to me. Ask the lone droplet that just settled on the tip of my lips to feel that *cacophony* of my senses without you. Yet the cuckoo says, in your absence begins a sweet lullaby in her heart.

You are not near me but always with me!

SHE

Isn't life like a vast sea beach and reminisces like those pebbles on sea beach! You can never have enough of them no matter how much you try to gather them!

So tonight, she came to her most cozy place; the safest place where she can just be, she; not what the world thinks of her. Night was silent but erupting memories within her were too boisterous in the wilderness of her solitude. She was celebrating the glory of love today. She blinked her eyes and looked outside the windows. The night was just like any other night.

Sometimes emotions play spoilsport in penning the right words at the right time. No, you can't always blame emotions. They have their own excuses and reasons. But quite often these are the words that are big time betrayers unwilling to settle on paper. In a world where emotions have become mere showpiece, relationships bloody trophies and conversations rather diplomatic, she chose to pause. She chose to step back and not be a part of the play.

She closed her eyes. Ah, darkness can be excruciating. She took a deep breathe and whispered, "Life is to be lived."

CONNECTIONS

The connection will always be there. Beyond space. Beyond time. Beyond this life and beyond silence. You won't realize but I will always remain connected with your thoughts like those hanging lichens.

Of the million distances that I have covered, I know, for one day, when the moon shall be on top of oceanic dark quilt, I will open the windows of my heart to let in the western winds touch the sensitive chords of my heart. Yeah, the heart that is embellished by Belgium glasses of royal palaces reflecting you eternally. Your one smile reflects on the walls of my heart a million times. So, you see, my love, this heart is nothing more than a mirror. It reflects what it gets.

Must be some day you might have loved me in your ignorance and to that day the shiny glasses have captured the love for a lifetime. I tell you the yearning is nothing but a replica of your love.

So, what if we ignore the love between us, the connection will always be there. With you and for you my connection was steadiest but forever the deepest one. And if one day I go on a monologue silence I will sleep in your reminisce. That night the western winds will steers me to your world and the connection between us will make you realize it was always us. Just you and me.
You. My ultimate abode

NUMBNESS

There are times in life when you have everything you love and live for by your side. Like that child's smile, family's happiness, friends, fun, humor, adventure, passion and success. The gorgeous sunset, the calm moon, stars, sea beach, hills, long roads, dreams, desires, you, your soul and what not!

And then in a *jiffy*, a luscious soft breeze with a delicate dew touch past you. You immediately rush to a lonely place; you want no one to be near you. Something chokes you from within. The breeze passes away but the dew drop clings to your eye lashes. You feel heavy within. You feel incomplete. The distant waves as though begin from your heart and reach the shores of your eyes. You don't make an effort to stop them, for you know in that moment they are untamable. Few seconds after you are okay. You come back. Upon asked where you went, you reply something went into your eyes. Life gets normal. Sigh!

SOLACE

Not often but sometimes on nights like this when a dew drop is just about to fall from the tip of a fresh virgin green leaf I do think of you till the dew drop falls on the ground and gets soaked. The night then turns magenta blue to fill my inkpot. During that era a muse takes birth. Clouds in my heart stand witness. Hey you, did it rain tonight in part of your world?!

Old things, old people, old memories and all that is old have a distinctive texture. They strike you and meet you in the most uninvited way. They do sometimes are corrosive by nature. But. When added with lubricant of silence, time and peace with self, they glare and their radiance lightens up our mind.

Tonight the solitude she so wanted whole her life was what she was given to make a journey inward, to walk through those gullies of fallen cedar and deodar leaves, to peep into those windows, benches, cupboards, sunsets, birds. To sit on that rock witnessing sunset, that shut gate, that wondering eyes waking up to see the sunrise, those vagabond scribblings , some poetry, some love etched in some part of sunken past in the unfathomable blue ocean of her unsaid words and thoughts! Gosh, she was turning clock backward. She was re-living all her memories again and creating art alive.

BUTTERFLY

You know how it is, that thing which we share is a itsy bitsy butterfly. Yes a butterfly, that flaps its wings and make way every night through the blowing windows and settle on the tip of the blank sheet of paper. The flickering pages get calmer. I watch that butterfly dancing to the tune I could never apprehend. It smiles back at me and tells me it is that tune which my heart often plays.

I wonder when silence is all I have where do the tune rise! I wonder in this hustle and bustle of fast paced life how the butterfly discovered my tune! But love, these days I want words, not any more of silence.

The butterfly then sits on my ring finger, hops to my thumb, and tells me, "Common lover, I am playing the piano; you just sing the song of your heart."

Thus, begins the orchestra. Moon plays the flute, the cuckoo for a change stands as an audience on the branch of that unknown tree, stars concatenate to rock their guitars in night's glory and as the symphony intensifies, I jot down the notes on the blank sheet of paper.

The butterfly then pauses and the entire universe gets mute.

"There it's done. Listen to the love song that often your heart plays, my lover. In silence there may be chaos. Love might be elusive in this chaotic silence. But remember the greatest glory of love shines in Rumi's mysticism, a lover's bewildered, eccentric and boisterous sentiments and that austere urge to be in oneness with beloved."

At the advent of dawn the butterfly disappears and as I wake up, I see the blank sheet of paper filled to brim.

HEART

I am reduced to poetry today in your raining reminisces. In the awe hours of a magenta twilight Faiz once mentioned, “O beloved do not ask me to love like the first love.” I smiled then.

The smile in that sultry magenta twilight has transformed to poetry today. The hour glass sand timer has invoked the epoch of virgin love. Today everything feels like your heart. The lone window, the cold breeze, the purple sky, the fresh lushes, the humming bird, the flattering butterflies, the thoughts of mermaids, the breath that enraptures these moments et al seem like your heart. But my beloved, do not ask me to love you like first love. The scars of hearts are too deep. I love you but not like the first time I loved you. I love you but not like being just yours.

Come, let's go to a place where I am your no-one and you are my nobody and that which is between you and me is nameless. Let's trade to a field sans bondage, walking free, no commitments to discharge and no promises to hold. Let today be my last day, so be with me like last time, last words, last gaze, and last hold. Be that ultimate smile to be exchanged between you and me, for when the sun shines tomorrow I shall break free. Hey you, let today be you, just you. Remember, I love you. Still do.

SYMPHONY

They tell writing is a willful act, the art that's crafted in the most delicate manner. Yet in some nights you wait ounce by ounce and words desert you in the best possible ways. Some thoughts are like a wild tigress impossible to tame. Your inkpot gets dry and immaculate sheets hesitate to be touched. The glass of tea gets empty but shivering lips wants more of it. You close your eyes. Ice cold silence. If rains tell stories then freezing cold hides many a tales. The deodar has shed its leaves. Rebirth is just about to begin. The dark clouds shadows the moon like quilt. It's time to undress the burning heart, unbutton the frozen soul and unfurl the just - lost - virgin lips and surrender to the quietude.

Mind today is a rocket and heart a mermaid. The rhythm says just to sail through it. So what there was turbulence, every storm promises calmness.

LONGING

Does my presence or absence matter to you? Do you ever miss me at the sight of flight of birds or when the breeze sings a lullaby while caressing your cheeks? I have often written letters to you in air and wanted them to fly to you. They say air can't be seen but felt. Do you ever in those feel heard my echo?

All my words have long been crest-fallen for they say nomads they are now, looking for a shade, to settle between you and me. But my love, distances have taken over intimacy between us. In some rainy nights those longing words take shelter under trees of remorse and in some sultry nights between shadows of the past. They have been now accustomed to a vagabond life like orphans, for it was only words to which we had given birth in our relationship.

Love was the moment when in that twilight the swarm left for the river and that foreign little bird chirped sitting on the branches stealing our glances and drawing our attention. Squirrels in their playful moods were playing hide and seek in between orchids and that mongoose couple was entwining each other in the glory of the aura.

I and you sat on that lone rock watching together sunset. I do sit today. The rock asks me about you. Last twilight I saw a petite rose growing up under the rocks nurtured by the tides of the sea standing tall against mighty winds. I didn't pluck it.

Love is watching the rose grow.

ASK ME NOT!

Dear Love, Do not ever ask who you are to me. Does the sea ever ask how it belongs to ocean? Does the moon ever ask the stars why they twinkle whole night without leaving the moon alone? Does the rainbow ever asks how it appears to the rain? Does the breeze ever ask the rustling leaves how they feel when it touch them? Does silence ask echo how they ever relate to each other? So, my love, I plead do not ask me who you are to me for love is discovering self and in your quest to love I shall find "Him" someday.

STORY

And you know on nights like this, in a state of relief and sigh, I sometime do think of you. It's eon now. But I think of you, the way you penned poems and I sought myself within those words. I was ignorant, not knowing that a poet never writes his/her story but only pens for readers to relate. You know since then I hold a story, a story of you.

But they tell I am a poet and your story remains untold.

I remember how desperate I was to learn from you and majestically you hinted me that this world is too cruel and it shall give me enough reasons to bleed and fill my inkpot.

And I learnt. I do think of you today. Yes, I think.

Times may change, people may take a back seat, memories of a long forgotten relationship may fade away, you may not think about it the same way as you did at some point of time, feelings may vary but one thing for sure is that no matter how busy life may get or you may move forward, once in a blue moon, just for once, the thin zephyr of reminiscence will definitely reverse way and touch, not you but your senses. Life will pause. Sepia moods. Whips of smile will begin from the hearth of heart, glimpse through your eyes and by the time it touches your immaculate lips you will be taken aback!

NIGHT

The pleasant feeling of night is that it fills the absence and emptiness quite so tactfully. It gifts a pillow to soak your tears, a lone window to answer your waiting, a moon to give company and darkness to get indiscernible from the world.

Tonight when you sleep wrap my thought on a sheet of paper and place it on your cushion adjacent to moon. Meanwhile I will spread the clouds as mattress extending to your doorways of left out world. When the moonbeam shines on the resplendent sheet of paper, do not question your dreams to where they bring you. You just walk on the clouds and gaze on the hanging stars of azure. Walk softly and steadily. The nightingale will sing that lullaby designed by the notes of my heart. Keep walking along the way of your dreams. Please.

As the dawn breaks, come back. Open that wrapped sheet of paper holding my thought. Read me- The Incomplete Me. So what? Sans a full stop, punctuated lines do have their identity. It's in those punctuations, you will know, how much I bled and was breathless.

ONCE

They say love can happen more than once.

I have often told my stories of love to them. Of varied kinds, of many plots, climax, suspense, romance, in poetry , with nature, with metaphors, similes, allegories, sonnets, drenched in rain, soaked in silence, in midst of chaos, in nothingness, in the boomerang of desires, bewildered thoughts, tumultuous plethora of emotions, in longings and cravings. I have done all of it to make them indulge in stories of love. Yes, love stories can happen more than once.

But.

Then.

When I take pauses, breathe uncomfortably, steal my looks, fumble, ignore lines between sharp pauses- I can't stop thinking of you! I know not why! True, that, Love may happen more than once. But "more than once" love happened to me manifold times but only with you. Let me put this way; never could I unstop myself falling for you. Love just happened.

Yes, Love just happens. But only once.

GRATITUDE

Of all the stories I bear in my heart, yours is my favorite; the one who sat near the window to catch a glimpse of the moon, the one who would wake up during midnight to pen bits of poetries, of the angel with wrath. How your words consoled my soul when I once broke up telling, "I tell you these tears often visit uninvited" and you replied, "Don't stop them tonight. Let them flow."

Every book begins from a gratitude note. But you knew the quintessential me, always struggling with words. How you smiled that day telling, "Who said words substantiate feelings. Let the silences interact."

True it is, life is bigger than words and silence is vaster than life. Yes, you are my favorite story, for you are the resplendent wisdom, destiny made me meet, in a once upon blue moon night. Actually I hold you more as a treasured wisdom than a story. When the world gets too high for me to comprehend, I see you walking into my dreams and guiding me to divine path.

Thank you for who you are and thank you for bringing the best out of me.

Solely Yours,
Mini Charmer

REALIZATION

It's strange how I only had a few words after you. I would make them settle on a nameless page and try to join the dots of stars. Every time I ended joining the dots, those words would have designed themselves in random orders. Closely when I held them, I saw you on the page. Tonight, they have abstained making me lonesome. I have searched them amidst echoes of my heart, silence in the caves, amidst cascading streams but sigh, they are nowhere to be traced. Do they hide beneath your pillows? You know, often my words have an old habit to sail to your island. No, not in a hope of your return. O, does the passing breeze ever turn back?

My words often peep into your windows. They say you still gaze at the moon; you pen some words in your black diary on your desk. That the love novel which made love knock at the doorstep of your heart still lies by your bed side, the Kashmiri quilt still veils you but lower to your heart. I know you still set your heart free and unveiled. Those words also do smile watching how the morning rays disturb your sleep. That they tell me you do, yes you do, sneak peek at me, like I do! But in my case, it's different. I tell my words to make sure all's fine with you. Don't know what your part of the story is? Its' okay some stories are better when left untold. Anyways these words have made me realized nothing much has changed. I, the inconsistent lover and you, the lingering imprint.

BECKON

Don't know why but everything today feels like you. Whole of May breeze blows me towards you. The summer warm path opens in your direction. The birds chirp your song. Don't know why? All I know is that I have given my accord to them. If it's you at the other end, let those "don't know why" take its course.

So Beloved, come, let's go to the other side. Let's give the day a miss. This world has been too dubious. Let's settle somewhere far from the monotony. let's lie for a while near the calm river, on the moistened earth, wrapped with the zephyr, under the sacred turquoise sky. Let no moon stare us, no stars we count, the sun also shall be veiled with the clouds. Yeah, you got it right, it should be a no-show day for all the celestials.

As we lie watching the vastness of azure, do not speak a word. They take most of the time. Instead, let nothing come between. Let's just take deep breathes and close our eyes. Shhh...No, let the moment head us to the cosmic moment.

I rest my pen here. Feel it. Are you feeling me?!!

DESIRES

“The idea of holidays is what keeps me going. Especially, when it’s about gifting a moment to someone to cherish for lifetime. You know what I like? The melodies of rising waves touching the beach, settling down and then returning. Reminds me of my journey."

(A pause and stoic silence.)

Breaking the silence lost in her thoughts she speaks, "When I was a kid, I always dreamt of having a home on the top of a hill ... away from city ... on the lap of nature. An open sky to fill the emptiness, breathing silence, handful of stars to lighten up the night, moon to glitter the lamp, hills to guard, the vast blankness lying ahead, the birds’ chirps to wake up to. Here I am, living my dream. If life is about rags to riches, then this is all about my story."

The author interrupts, “It’s not just a story. It’s your success story.”

She then peeps out of the window, watching the boys of her gullies playing.

“Train is a journey to mystics. The churning sounds of iron wheels, the little girl’s music ‘*train gadi chuk chuk*’, those dark tunnel beyond which there is mist and fog all around and above all of it, the smoke of steam engine mingling with the mists revoking an old era. A poetess then picks up her suitcase and peeps out of the iron bar of the train. She stands stupefied witnessing the pristine, immaculate earth having a shower on milk tub of fog and mists.

Hmmm.... There is something very mystics about winter train. Not every station is a destination. Sometimes the journey also becomes a destination. May be that's how travelers are born."

The author uncapped his pen. A story was about to take birth from the author's pen.

QUESTION-II

You know how it is to love exactly? Do you have any idea? I tell you it's not easy because every morning I wake up falling in love with you and every night I sleep realizing that when I wake up the moon shall be nowhere to be seen.

Under the vast azure I have often drawn your many shapes with each star telling an unusual story. Story of how we began, how we ended and how we began to end or ended to begin all over again. Do you understand what it takes to love?

They say if you are love then nothing can stop you from being in love. I have no idea how your love has turned to be an ocean which seems to have depths but no ends. Often in eclipses I have rose high under your mystifying allure. On other quiet nights, like pendulum, I have often tussled to and fro of 'what was' and 'what could have been' between you and me.

Your hope of advent is like that distant firework which often crackle and frizzles and later falls like a shooting star. O yeah, I shouldn't. I shouldn't hope for your return. So, these days when spring asks your whereabouts, I craft you into an art. The spring often express its grudge telling art has no form and I reply apprehensively when did I and your love ever had a form!

If silence is your essence, I want to be that deep breath you take in hour of nothingness. If love is that bosom that lighten up your smiles, then I will be the dalia of your canvas and if ever there is a poem which makes your heart skip a bit faster, then I will be those ellipses that shall linger in your senses forever. Yeah forever, for with you, I know nothing less than forever.

SENTENCES

Words fuse to create sentences. Some complete. Some incomplete and some waiting to begin or waiting for a completion. You and I met without any of them. They say some stories don't have a language. Then what language does a sentence speaks.

Of emotions? Of feelings? Of silences? Of expressions?

Perhaps of breaths! No, sometimes of breathlessness. Like that lump in throat. Like those hands of clock that moved too fast when we had to bid goodbye.

Irony is a word contains a sentence within it.

But.

Life.

Love.

Goodbye.

The sentence may remain as it is, but pages once penned shall never remain the same.

Period.

MONOLOGUE

The turquoise sky today opens like a bridge where at one end stands you and at farther end is my tryst with unreachable you. Clouds remain mysterious until it rains. Once it rains, they just flow. The essence of mysticism on a cloud filled dusk gheraos the aura and lightens the bonfires in my heart. It fizzles, sparks, blazes the whims and fantasies of an unrequited affair that ended long before it could begin.

Love, the wise say, is a waste of time and trust, is a blind man's business. It echoes then in the world of utopia, "No trust, and no love." The dusk goes dark as the vampire engulfs the blooded moon. The whimsical heart dies many a death before it shrinks and sinks ultimately.

Uh, life! The only thing I was sure in my life was that I was so bloody unsure about you!

ELIXIR OF LIFE

I have kept you in some corner of my heart like that red feather I stored in some page of notebook. I should have disowned you, they say, because letting go off old creates space for new. But when I didn't let go off anything when you created a space in my life, then why let go off you, to make space for new?

You are but a healing space, a smile that emanates from heart and sparkle through lips, my out-for-a-while space to redeem my sanity when there is too much chaos around, a space of my being.

So, tell me, is it worth to bargain all for new? Let the new create space by its own like you did. This is my heart, not a customized shelf. I believe love is a world. It's not a space. It makes space, not looks for space. Hey you, let you embellish in some corner of my heart forever. Remember, I promised you togetherness. My word is my existence. Period.

GOODBYE

Nobody knows the story you have lived, that tear which fell from one eye, that cup which was left halfway, that stare which never promised an eternity, that wait which never had any signs of return, that discussion/argument which ended with silence, that gullies which let your heart be child all over again.... nobody knows that story.

Sometimes that pain in someone's heart, look in someone's eyes, silence in someone's thought and slight chuckle from someone's corner of lips will tell how much they have loved someone. Sadly, those love stories either never began or is left unsaid/ unheard.

Of all the years I have known you, of the bits and pieces I gathered of you, I will bead them in a story. A story of me, you have no idea about; of the part of mine I discovered when I was with you, of all that I went through and much more than what your mind could ever comprehend. I will backpack them in my memory and fly away to a far stretched out island. I shall also bring along with me my other stories too. Far away I shall discover a stranger for a twilight and unravel all my stories. When the sea and shores meet, I will let down my guards and feel light. That's how I will actually let go off you.

You know what, love makes one so vulnerable and so was I, stuck with Cupid arrows. Sigh, you will never know many such fond stories about you that my mind carries! You will never know. Period.

NOTES

NOTES

NOTES

NOTES